In the tub

Story by Barbara Stavetski

Illustrations by Mark Weber

Dr. Judith Nadell, Series Editor

I put in the water.

I put in the bubbles.

I put in the soap.

I put in the sponge.

I put in the duck.

I put in the boat.

I put in the frog.

I put in **me**!